MOTHER GOOSE

Illustrated by Marguerite K. Scott

A Golden Book · New York

Western Publishing Company, Inc.
Racine, Wisconsin 53404

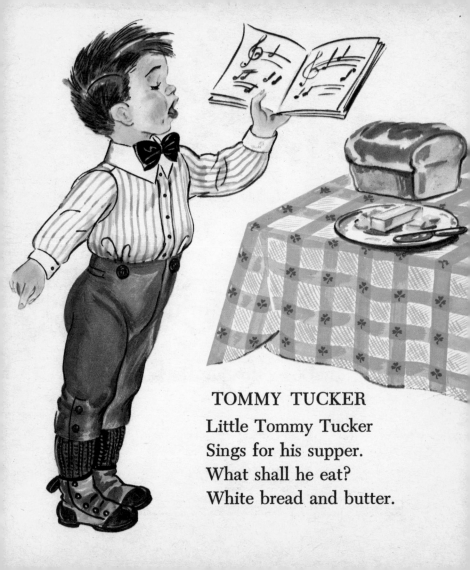

TOMMY TUCKER

Little Tommy Tucker
Sings for his supper.
What shall he eat?
White bread and butter.

LITTLE BO-PEEP

Little Bo-Peep has lost her sheep
    And can't tell where to find them;
Leave them alone, and they'll come home
    And bring their tails behind them.

LITTLE MISS LILY

Little Miss Lily, you're dreadfully silly
    To wear such a very long skirt.
If you take my advice, you will hold it up nice
    And not let it trail in the dirt.

PETER, PETER, PUMPKIN EATER

Peter, Peter, pumpkin eater,
Had a wife and couldn't keep her.
He put her in a pumpkin shell,
And there he kept her very well.

BOBBY SHAFTOE

Bobby Shaftoe's gone to sea,
Silver buckles on his knee;
He'll come back and marry me,
Pretty Bobby Shaftoe.

RIDE, BABY, RIDE

Ride, baby, ride; pretty baby shall ride
And have a little puppy dog tied to her side
And a little pussycat tied to the other,
And away she shall go to see her grandmother,
To see her grandmother, to see her grandmother.

MOLLY AND I

Molly, my sister, and I fell out,
And what do you think it was all about?
I loved coffee and she loved tea,
And that was the reason we couldn't agree.

THERE WAS A LITTLE GIRL

There was a little girl who had a little curl
  Right in the middle of her forehead.
When she was good, she was very, very good,
  But when she was bad, she was horrid.

THE OLD WOMAN
WHO LIVED IN A SHOE

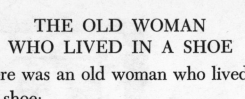

There was an old woman who lived in
a shoe;
She had so many children, she
didn't know what to do.

She gave them some broth without any bread;
She whipped them all soundly and sent them
    to bed.

MARY HAD A PRETTY BIRD

Mary had a pretty bird.
Feathers bright and yellow,
Slender legs—upon my word,
He was a pretty fellow.
The sweetest notes he always sang,
Which much delighted Mary;
And near the cage she'd ever sit
To hear her own canary.

A BOY IN THE BARN

A little boy went into a barn
And lay down on some hay.
An owl came out and flew about,
And the little boy ran away.

LITTLE BOY BLUE

Little Boy Blue,
   come blow your horn;
The sheep's in the meadow,
   the cow's in the corn.
Where's the boy who looks
   after the sheep?
He's under the haystack, fast asleep.

JACK AND JILL

Jack and Jill went up the hill
To fetch a pail of water;
Jack fell down and cracked his crown,
And Jill came tumbling after.

Then up Jack got and home did trot
As fast as he could caper.
They put him to bed and plastered his head
With vinegar and brown paper.

DEEDLE, DEEDLE, DUMPLING

Deedle, deedle, dumpling, my son John
Went to bed with his stockings on;
One shoe off and one shoe on,
Deedle, deedle, dumpling, my son John.

LITTLE GIRL, LITTLE GIRL

Little girl, little girl, where have you been?
Gathering roses to give to the Queen.
Little girl, little girl, what gave she you?
She gave me a diamond as big as my shoe.

JUMPING JOAN

Here am I, little jumping Joan.
When nobody's with me, I'm always alone.

HANDY PANDY

Handy Pandy, Jack-a-dandy,
Loves plum cake and sugar candy.
He bought some at a grocer's shop,
And out he came, hop, hop, hop!

DANCE, LITTLE BABY

Dance, little baby, dance up high!
Never mind, baby, Mother is by.
Crow and caper, caper and crow;
There, little baby, there you go!

Up to the ceiling, down to the ground,
Backward and forward, round and round.
Dance, little baby, and Mother will sing,
With a merry chorale, ding, ding, ding!

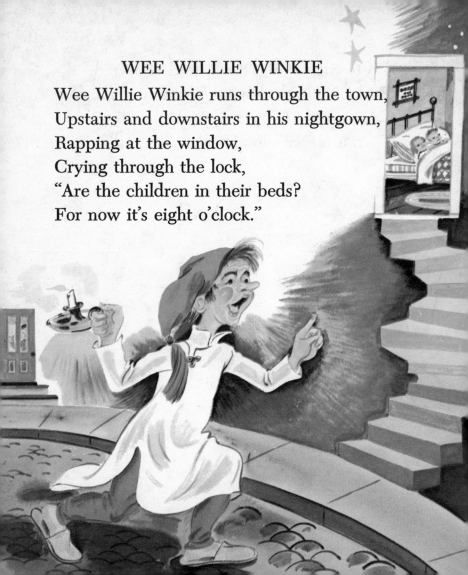

WEE WILLIE WINKIE

Wee Willie Winkie runs through the town,
Upstairs and downstairs in his nightgown,
Rapping at the window,
Crying through the lock,
"Are the children in their beds?
For now it's eight o'clock."

LITTLE MISS MUFFET

Little Miss Muffet
Sat on a tuffet,
Eating her curds and whey.
There came a great spider
Who sat down beside her
And frightened Miss Muffet away.

THERE WAS A CROOKED MAN

There was a crooked man,
   and he went a crooked mile;
He found a crooked sixpence
   against a crooked stile.

He bought a crooked cat,
   which caught a crooked mouse,
And they all lived together
   in a little crooked house.

BYE, BABY BUNTING

Bye, Baby Bunting,
Daddy's gone a-hunting
To get a little rabbit skin
To wrap his Baby Bunting in.